This Book Belongs to

_____

A Children's Treasury of
Nursery Rhymes

Illustrations by
Linda Bleck

STERLING CHILDREN'S BOOKS
New York

Hey Diddle Diddle

Hey diddle diddle,
The cat and the fiddle,
The cow jumped over the moon.
The little dog laughed to see such sport,
And the dish ran away with the spoon.

Little Boy Blue

Little Boy Blue, come blow your horn,
The sheep's in the meadow, the cow's in the corn.
Where is the boy who looks after the sheep?
He's under a haystack, fast asleep.
Will you wake him? No, not I,
For if I do, he's sure to cry.

Little Bo Peep

Little Bo Peep has lost her sheep
And doesn't know where to find them.
Leave them alone and they'll come home,
Wagging their tails behind them.

Georgie Porgie

Georgie Porgie, pudding and pie,
Kissed the girls and made them cry.
When the boys came out to play,
Georgie Porgie ran away.

Diddle, Diddle, Dumpling

Diddle, diddle, dumpling,
My son John.
Went to bed
With his trousers on.
One shoe off
And one shoe on!
Diddle, diddle, dumpling,
My son John!

Jack and Jill

Jack and Jill went up the hill
To fetch a pail of water.
Jack fell down and broke his crown
And Jill came tumbling after.

Up Jack got, and home did trot
As fast as he could caper.
He went to bed and bound his head
With vinegar and brown paper.

Little Miss Muffet

Little Miss Muffet sat on a tuffet,
Eating her curds and whey.
Along came a spider,
Who sat down beside her,
And frightened Miss Muffet away.

Hickory, Dickory, Dock

Hickory, dickory, dock! The mouse ran up the clock! The clock struck one, the mouse ran down. Hickory, dickory, dock!

One, Two, Buckle My Shoe

One, two, buckle my shoe.

Three, four,
knock at the door.

Five, six,
pick up sticks.
Seven, eight,
lay them straight.

Nine, ten, a big fat hen.

Eleven, twelve, dig and delve.

Thirteen, fourteen, maids a-courting.
Fifteen, sixteen, maids in the kitchen.

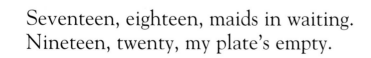

Seventeen, eighteen, maids in waiting.
Nineteen, twenty, my plate's empty.

Old King Cole

Old King Cole was a merry old soul,
And a merry old soul was he.
He called for his pipe,
And he called for his bowl,
And he called for his fiddlers three.

Every fiddler had a fiddle fine,
And a very fine fiddle had he, had he.
Tweedle dum, tweedle dee,
Went the fiddlers three.

Oh, there's none so rare
As can compare
With King Cole and his fiddlers three.

The Queen of Hearts

The Queen of Hearts,
She made some tarts,
All on a summer's day.
The Knave of Hearts,
He stole the tarts
And took them clean away.

The King of Hearts,
Called for the tarts
And beat the Knave full sore.
The Knave of Hearts
Brought back the tarts
And vowed he'd steal no more.

Sing a Song of Sixpence

Sing a song of sixpence,
A pocket full of rye.
Four-and-twenty blackbirds
Baked in a pie.
When the pie was opened,
They all began to sing.
Now, wasn't that a dainty dish
To set before the king?

The king was in his countinghouse,
Counting out his money.
The queen was in the parlor
Eating bread and honey.
The maid was in the garden,
Hanging out the clothes.
Along there came a big black bird
And pecked off her nose!

Humpty Dumpty

Humpty Dumpty sat on the wall,
Humpty Dumpty had a great fall.
All the king's horses, and all the king's men,
Couldn't put Humpty together again.

Jack Sprat

Jack Sprat could eat no fat,
His wife could eat no lean.
And so betwixt the two of them
They licked the platter clean.

Pease Porridge Hot

Pease porridge hot!
Pease porridge cold!
Pease porridge in the pot
Nine days old.
Some like it hot,
Some like it cold,
I like it in the pot
Nine days old!

Jack, Be Nimble

Jack, be nimble,
Jack, be quick,
Jack, jump over
The candlestick.

Jack jumped high,
Jack jumped low,
Jack jumped over
And burned his toe.

Old Mother Hubbard

Old Mother Hubbard
Went to the cupboard
To get her poor dog a bone.
But when she got there,
The cupboard was bare,
And so the poor dog had none.

Little Jack Horner

Little Jack Horner
Sat in a corner
Eating his Christmas pie.
He put in his thumb
And pulled out a plum
And said, "What a good boy am I."

This Little Piggy

This little piggy went to market,
This little piggy stayed home.
This little piggy had roast beef,
This little piggy had none.
And this little piggy cried,
"Wee, wee, wee,"
All the way home.

There Was an Old Lady Who Lived in a Shoe

There was an old lady who lived in a shoe.
She had so many children, she didn't know what to do.
She gave them some broth,
Without any bread,
Kissed them all softly and sent them to bed.

Rub-a-Dub-Dub

Rub-a-dub-dub,
Three men in a tub,
And how do you think they got there?
The butcher, the baker, the candlestick maker,
They all jumped out of a rotten potato!
'Twas enough to make a man stare.

Mary, Mary, Quite Contrary

Mary, Mary, quite contrary,
How does your garden grow?
With silver bells and cockleshells
And pretty maids all in a row.

For my children, David and Sarah. —L.B.

STERLING CHILDREN'S BOOKS
New York

An Imprint of Sterling Publishing
387 Park Avenue South
New York, NY 10016

STERLING CHILDREN'S BOOKS and the distinctive
Sterling Children's Books logo are trademarks of Sterling Publishing Co., Inc.
Paperback edition published in 2014.
Previously published by Sterling Publishing Co., Inc. in a different format in 2006.

© 2006 by Sterling Publishing Co., Inc.
Illustrations © 2006 by Linda Bleck
Design by Josh Simons, Simonsays Design!

ISBN 978-1-4549-1359-7

Library of Congress Cataloging-in-Publication Data

A children's treasury of nursery rhymes / illustrations by Linda Bleck.
    p. cm.
 Summary: An illustrated collection of well-known nursery rhymes.
 ISBN-13: 978-1-4027-2980-5
 ISBN-10: 1-4027-2980-4
 1. Nursery rhymes. 2. Children's poetry. [1. Nursery rhymes.] I. Bleck, Linda, ill.
PZ8.3.C43453 2006
[E]—dc22

2005034079

Distributed in Canada by Sterling Publishing
c/o Canadian Manda Group, 165 Dufferin Street
Toronto, Ontario, Canada M6K 3H6
Distributed in the United Kingdom by GMC Distribution Services
Castle Place, 166 High Street, Lewes, East Sussex, England BN7 1XU
Distributed in Australia by Capricorn Link (Australia) Pty. Ltd.
P.O. Box 704, Windsor, NSW 2756, Australia

For information about custom editions, special sales, premium and corporate purchases,
please contact Sterling Special SalesDepartment at 800-805-5489 or specialsales@sterlingpub.com.

Printed in China
Lot #
2 4 6 8 10 9 7 5 3
12/18

www.sterlingpublishing.com/kids